Crystal Bowman

'06

My ABC Bible

Written by
Crystal Bowman

Illustrated by
Stacey Lamb

Zonderkidz

Aa

A is for the ANIMALS
Walking two by two.
See the pair of hippos
And the hoppity kangaroo?

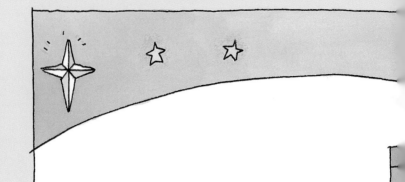

B is for BETHLEHEM,
Where Jesus Christ was born.
See him in the manger
So cozy and warm?

Cc

C is for the COLORFUL COAT
That Joseph wore each day.
His brothers all were jealous
So they sent him far away.

Dd

D is for brave DANIEL
Who prayed each day and night.
They fed him to the lions
But the lions didn't bite.

Ee

E is for ELIJAH,
A man who didn't die.
A chariot of fire
Whooshed him through the sky.

F is for FIERY FURNACE.
See the red hot flame.
Some men of God were thrown inside.
But soon the angel came.

Gg

G is for GOLIATH,
The giant big and strong.
He thought he was the mighty one,
But he was very wrong!

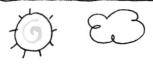

Hh

H is for dear HANNAH
Who prayed to God each day.
Then God gave her a baby boy.
God listens when we pray.

Ii

I is for ISAAC,
The son of Abraham.
They traveled to the altar,
Then God supplied a lamb.

J j

J is for JESUS,
The son God sent to earth.
Every year at Christmastime
We celebrate his birth.

Kk

K is for the royal KINGS
Who traveled very far.
Bringing gifts of gold and myrrh
While following the star.

L is for LAZARUS.
His friends thought he was dead.
Jesus brought him back to life.
"Arise, arise!" he said.

Mm

M is for MARY
The mother of God's Son.
An angel said to Mary,
"You are the favored one."

Nn

N is for the fishermen's NETS
As full as they can be.
Jesus said, "Now leave your NETS.
Come and follow me!"

O is for the widow's OIL,
filling every jar.
She only had a little bit,
But it went very far.

Pp

P is for the awful PLAGUES –
Locust, frogs, and flies.
God sent the PLAGUES to Egypt
Because of Pharaoh's lies.

Qq

Q is for QUEEN Esther,
The young and lovely QUEEN,
Who saved the Jewish people
From Haman's evil scheme.

Rr

R is for the pretty RAINBOW
See it up above,
Shining brightly in the sky
Showing us God's love?

Ss

S is for the STORIES
That Jesus loved to tell.
All the little children
Listened very well.

T t

T is for the TEMPLE
Where people went each day
To bring their gifts and offerings.
To worship God and pray.

U is for the UPPER ROOM
Where Jesus' friends would eat,
They'd listen to his teaching
And wash each other's feet.

Vv

V is for the VILLAGES
Where Jesus healed the sick.
The blind could see,
The deaf could hear,
The lame could run and kick!

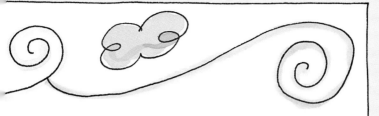

Ww

W is for the WINDS and WAVES
That rocked the little boat.
Jesus stopped the mighty storm
And kept the boat afloat.

X is for EXCITED!
Hear the people cry,
"Hosanna in the highest!
Our Lord is passing by!"

Yy

Y is just for YOU.
Jesus loves YOU so.
Share his love with all your friends,
Tell everyone you know.

Zz

Z is for ZACCHAEUS
Who climbed up in a tree.
When Jesus saw ZACCHAEUS
He said, "Have lunch with me!"

Now you know the ALPHABET
And Bible stories too.
Say the letters A to Z,
It's very fun to do!

The End.

My ABC Bible/My ABC Prayers
Copyright © 2001 by Crystal Bowman
Illustrations copyright © 2001 by Stacey Lamb
Requests for information should be addressed to:

Zonder**kidz**™
The children's group of Zondervan

Grand Rapids, Michigan 49530
www.zonderkidz.com

Zonderkidz is a trademark of Zondervan.

ISBN: 0310-70160-0

Editors: Mary McNeil; Gwen Ellis
Art direction and design: Michelle Lenger

Printed in China

02 03 04 /HK/ 5 4 3 2

All done, bye-bye!

Now you know the alphabet
And many prayers to pray.
The letters here are all mixed up
How many can you say?

Z is for ZEBRA

Thank you for the ZEBRA,
And elephant at the zoo.
The lion and the tiger,
Each one was made by you.

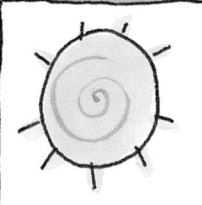

Yy

Y is for YARD

Lord, I like my great big YARD
Where I can run around.
Thank you for the soft, green grass
That grows up from the ground.

X is for XYLOPHONE

I like to play my XYLOPHONE,
I like to sing along.
Thank you, God, for music,
And for a happy song.

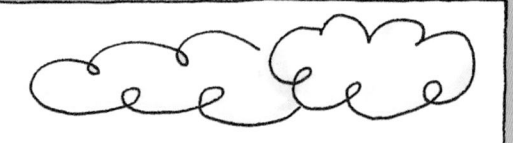

W is for WATER

Thank you for WATER
to wash my hands,
And WATER for ships at sea.
When I am thirsty and need a drink,
I'm glad you made WATER for me.

Potato

V is for VEGETABLES

For corn to munch and
carrots to crunch,
For potatoes creamy and white,
Thank you, God,
for VEGETABLES
That give me strength and might.

U is for UNIVERSE

God you made the UNIVERSE,
The world and outer space.
And everything that you have made
You keep right in its place.

T is for TOES

From my head down to my TOES,
You made each part of me.
Thank you, Lord, that I can dance,
And smell and touch and see.

Ss

S is for SUN

Thank you, Father, for the SUN
That makes me warm inside,
Thank you for the sunny days
So I can swing and slide.

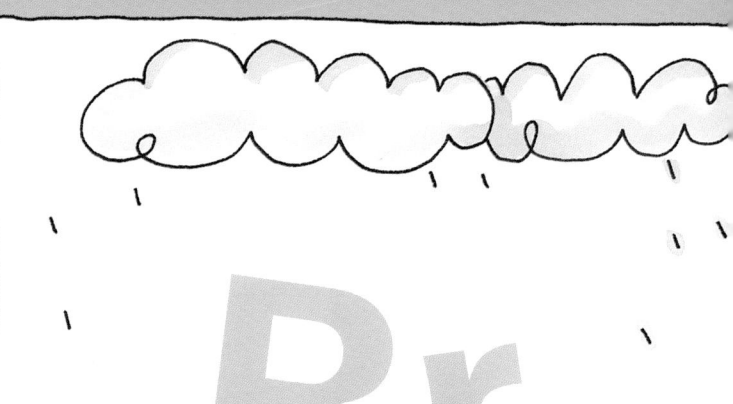

R is for RAIN

Lord, I praise you for the RAIN
That makes the rivers flow.
Thank you for the RAIN you send
To help the flowers grow.

Q is for QUIET

When I am QUIET
I whisper a prayer,
When I am QUIET I rest.
Thank you, God, for QUIET times;
Sometimes QUIET is best.

P is for PARENTS

Thank you for my PARENTS
Who teach me wrong from right,
Who make my meals and
wash my clothes
And tuck me in at night.

O is for ONE

There's just ONE God who loves me
There's just ONE God who cares.
There's just ONE God in heaven
Who listens to my prayers.

Nn

N is for NIGHT

Lord, I thank you for the NIGHT,
  And for the moon so high.
I praise you for the tiny stars
  That twinkle in the sky.

Mm

M is for MOUTH

My MOUTH can sing your praises.
My MOUTH can say a prayer.
My MOUTH can say,
"I love you, Lord,"
Anytime and anywhere.

L is for LOVE

God, I know you LOVE me.
You LOVE my family too.
Thank you, Father, for your LOVE,
A special gift from you.

K is for KEEP

Father, KEEP me in your sight,
KEEP me safe and strong.
KEEP me from temptation,
And doing what is wrong.

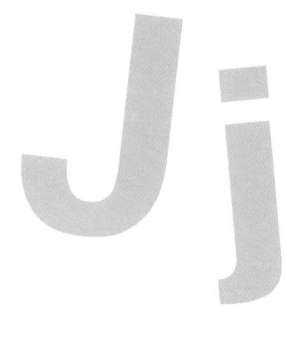

J is for JOY

Thank you, God, for times to giggle.
For times of fun and JOY.
Thank you for the happy days
You give each girl and boy.

Ii

I is for INTO

Dear Lord Jesus, hear my prayer
Please come INTO my heart.
Fill me with your peace and love
Come INTO every part.

H is for HOUSE

Thank you, Father, for my HOUSE
That keeps me safe and warm
When it's cold and rainy,
Or through a winter storm.

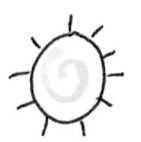

Gg

G is for GOD

GOD, you are great and mighty.
GOD, you are good and kind.
I praise you, GOD, for who you are
With all my heart and mind.

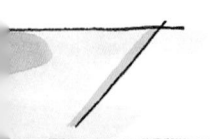

F is for FOOD

Bless this FOOD, dear Lord I pray,
And as I bow my head,
I thank you for delicious FOOD
For fruit and milk and bread.

Ee

E is for EARS

Thank you, God, for EARS to hear
The words that grown-ups say.
Help me, Lord, to listen,
And help me to obey.

Dd

D is for DOCTORS

Thank you, God, for DOCTORS
Who help me when I'm sick,
Who give me special medicine
So I feel better quick.

C is for CREATION

For birds and trees and bumblebees,
And mountains great and tall,
We praise you for CREATION
For you have made it all.

B is for BED

Lord you know just what I need.
Thank you for my BED
Where I can rest a little while,
And lay my sleepy head.

Aa

A is for ANGELS

Thank you, God, for ANGELS
That keep me safe each day,
In the house or in the yard,
When I run out to play.

My ABC Prayers

Written by
Crystal Bowman

Illustrated by
Stacey Lamb

Zonderkidz